"Stand Back,"
said the Elephant,
"I'm Going to Sneeze!"

Patricia Thomas

"Stand Back," said the Elephant, "I'm Going to Sneeze!"

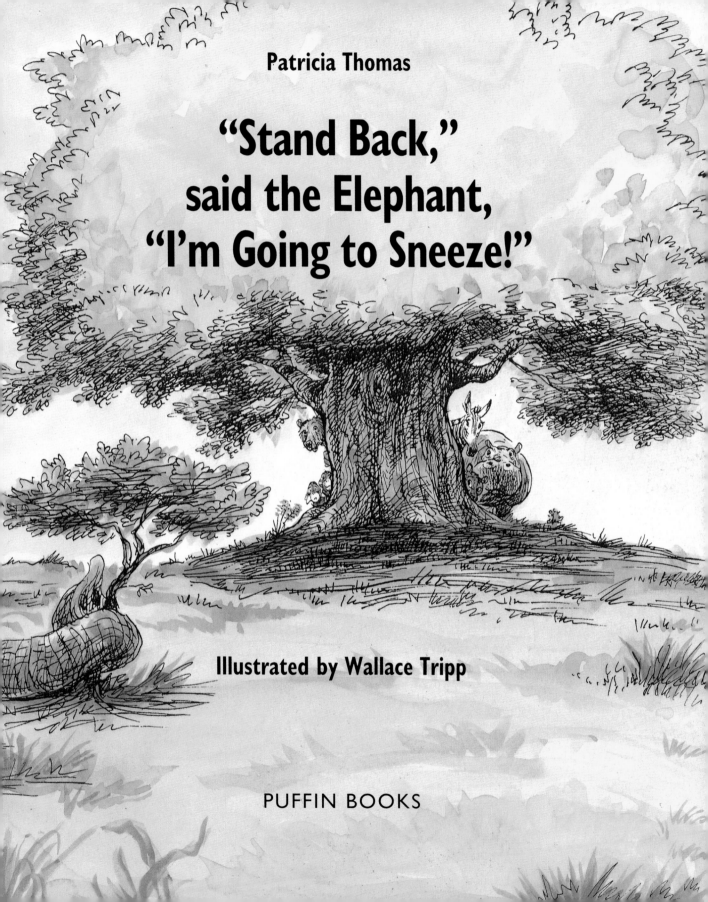

Illustrated by Wallace Tripp

PUFFIN BOOKS

"Stand back," said the elephant,
"I'm going to sneeze!
I hate to alarm you,
But I don't wish to harm you.
My friends, I fear
It's clear....
Oh, dear,
You'd better stand back, I'm going to sneeze."

"Oh no, oh no!"
Cried the buffalo.
"You're so big and strong
And your trunk is so long,
Your sneezes send everyone flying along,
Bumping and thumping down pathway and trail,
Bouncing and jouncing head over tail,
Tumbling and bumbling. . . .
Your sneeze is a gale . . .
Or a hurricane!
I hate to complain,
But please,
Don't sneeze!"

"No, no, please,
Don't sneeze,"
Cried the monkeys in the trees.
"You make such a breeze
When you sneeze.
The last time you blew us right out of the trees.
The branches began to bend and to sway
And some of us landed so far away
We didn't get back until the next day.

The leaves all went whirling
And tumbling and swirling,
And the flowers
Shook for hours
The last time you sneezed.
Even a cough
Would knock some of us off.
Oh, *please*,
Don't sneeze!"

With a shriek
The parrot opened his beak.
"The elephant says he's going to sneeze!"

"Oh, Elephant, please!" cried the birds in the trees.
"The last time you sneezed we lost every feather.
We didn't know whether
We'd ever get back together.
Every parakeet
Was bare as a sheet
From his head to his feet.
What's more, all the whales
Had peacocks' tails,
And the wings of the cockatoo
Were stuck on the kangaroo.
You must confess
It was quite a mess,
Very confusing
And not too amusing.
Even a snuffle
Makes our feathers ruffle.
Oh, *please*,
Don't sneeze!"

"Fly, fly," called the birds to the bees.
"The elephant says he's going to sneeze!"

"Oh, no," buzzed the bees.
"Not a sneeze! Not a sneeze!
The last time he blew off our stings
As well as our wings,
And we had to make do
With rose thorns and glue.

Furthermore…what a shock…
We all had to walk…
On our knees,
If you please,
(And that's hard on bees' knees)…
While our wings grew back in.
What a sin!
Oh, *please,*
Don't sneeze!"

"Beware, beware,"
 Called the bees to the bear.
"The elephant says he's going to sneeze."

"Oh, please,
 Not a sneeze,"
 Cried the bear.
"That's not fair.
 I declare,
 The last time he sneezed he blew off all my hair,
 And left me so bare
 I spent the whole winter in long underwear—
 Nothing's so sad as a bear that is bare.
 The poor giraffe
 (Don't laugh)
 Almost bent in half,
 And the crocodile's snout
 Was turned inside out
 The last time he sneezed.
 A sniff or a snuff
 Is bad enough...
 But a sneeze!
 Oh, *please*,
 Don't sneeze!"

"I don't suppose
You could hold your nose,
Or wait awhile?"
Asked the crocodile
With a sad little smile.

"Oh my,
Do try,"
Said the fly.

"We wish,"
Said the fish,
"You would
If you could.
The last time you blew off all of our scales
From our heads to our tails,
And our gills
Got the chills,
Our skin
Is so thin.
If you do it again
We'll freeze!
Oh, *please*,
Don't sneeze!"

The zebra yelled, "Yipes,
You'll blow off my stripes,
Plus lots and lots
Of the leopard's spots,
And all of the snakes will be tied up in knots!"

The hippopotamus
Said, "A lot of us
Will fall right on our bottom-us
If you sneeze.
So *please*,
Don't sneeze."

"I'm sorry, my friends," said the elephant sadly.
"About all of this I do feel badly.
 If I could keep from sneezing I'd do it gladly.
 But I have such a twitch
 In my trunk, and an itch,
 Plus a bit of a tickle,
 And even a prickle.

You must run, fly, and hop.
I'm afraid I can't stop.
I would
If I could,
But there's nothing to do....
Ah...
Ah...."

"BOO!"
Shouted a little brown mouse
Jumping out of his house.
He stood right up on his little tiptoes,
Stuck out his tongue, and wiggled his nose.

"Eek!" shouted the elephant, jumping up in the air.
"That's a mouse! That's a mouse standing there!
I must hide in a tree
Before he gets me
Or jump in the lake.
For goodness' sake!
Don't scare me!
Please spare me!"

The mouse laughed. "Oh, pooh!
Now what could I do?
A little thing like me to a big thing like you?
I only wanted to give you a scare,
And it worked as sure as you're standing there.
Elephant, think about it, please!
You completely forgot to sneeze!"

"Well, what do you know?"
Cried the elephant. "That's so!
It's astounding,
Confounding.
As I live and breathe!
I don't think I really have to sneeze."
He began to giggle. "He, he, he, he!
That's the funniest thing that has happened to me!
Ha, ha, ha! Ho, ho, ho!"
The elephant shook from his head to his toe.
He ho-hoed and ha-haed.
He giggled and guffawed.
He chortled and chuckled
Until his knees buckled.

He sat down and rolled from side to side.
In fact, the elephant laughed till he cried.
He laughed till the ground was shivering and shaking
And all of the trees were quivering and quaking.
The monkeys came tumbling out of the trees,
And the stings fell off every one of the bees.
The bird's feathers went flying
To goodness-knows-where,

And all of the hair
Fell off the bear.

The giraffe
Bent in half,
And the crocodile's snout
Turned inside out.
The fish lost their scales
From their heads to their tails.

The zebra yelled, "Yipes!
There go my stripes!"
While the hippo went *thump*
Right on his plump . . . you-know-what!

And into a puddle
The mouse went . . . *ker-plop!*
Then he sat up and shouted,
"This simply must stop!
We're terribly glad you don't have to sneeze,
But if you must laugh, laugh SOFTLY.
Oh, Elephant, *please!*"